GROUNDWOOD BOOKS

HOUSE OF ANANSI PRESS

TORONTO BERKELEY

Sarah Withrow

Be a

Baby

PICTURES BY Manuel Monroy

Be a birdie, Baby.
Be a lonely loon.

Or be a bowl of pudding and
I'll eat you with a spoon.

Be a hungry monkey,
shove bananas in your mouth.

Or be a herd of elephants and
I'll chase you round the house.

Be a blaring siren.
Be a fan that whirrs.

Be a big-vroom motorbike
or a shaggy dog that purrs.

Be a dancing flower.
Be a tired tree.

Or be a cloud up in the sky
and make it rain on me.

But if you rain on me, please,
then be a soft warm breeze.

Won't you be a gentle breeze
for poor old rained-on me?

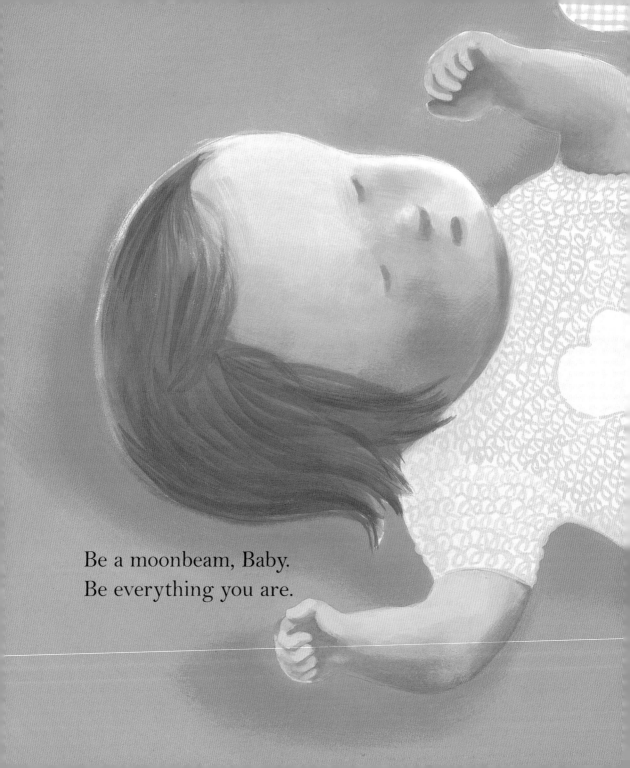

Be a moonbeam, Baby.
Be everything you are.

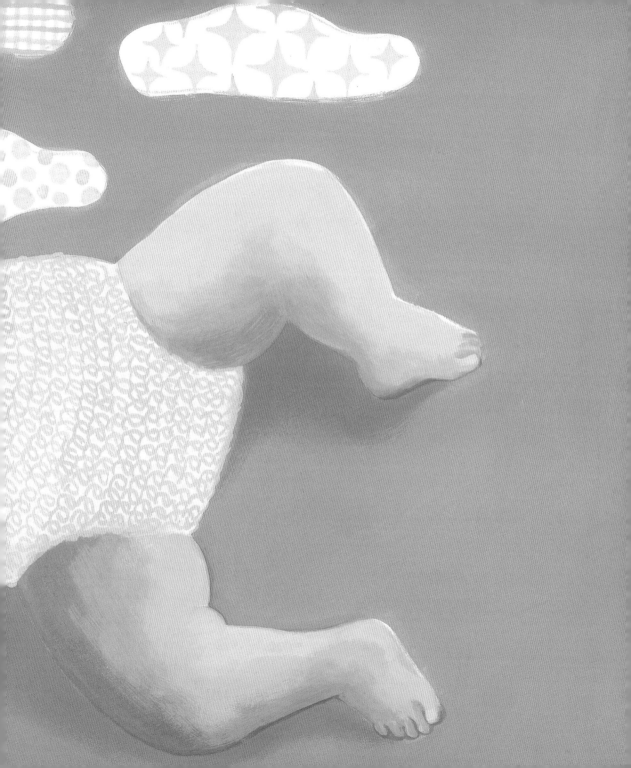

And I'll toss you to the sky top
to meet the northern star.

Or be a baby, Baby,
and I'll bundle you up tight.
And I'll rock you in my arms
until the night turns light.

Groundwood Books / House of Anansi Press
110 Spadina Avenue, Suite 801
Toronto, Ontario M5V 2K4

Distributed in the USA by Publishers Group West
1700 Fourth Street, Berkeley, CA 94710

ONTARIO ARTS COUNCIL
CONSEIL DES ARTS DE L'ONTARIO

We acknowledge for their financial support of our publishing program the Canada Council for the Arts, the Government of Canada through the Book Publishing Industry Development Program (BPIDP) and the Ontario Arts Council.

Library and Archives Canada Cataloguing in Publication
Withrow, Sarah
Be a Baby / by Sarah Withrow; pictures by Manuel Monroy.
ISBN-13: 978-0-88899-776-0
ISBN-10: 0-88899-776-0
1. Lullabies, Canadian (English). 2. Children's poetry, Canadian (English). I. Monroy, Manuel II. Title.
PS8595.I8455B42 2007   jC811'.54   C2007-900606-X

The illustrations were done in gouache.
Design by Michael Solomon
Printed and bound in China